Best

Friends

Hot Gay Romance Erotica

CHRIS JOHNS

WARNING

This book contains sexually explicit scenes and adult language. It may be considered offensive to some readers. This book is for sale to adults ONLY.

* * * * * * * * * * * * * * * * * * *

Please store your files wisely where they cannot be accessed by underage readers.

Please feel free to send me an email. Just know that these emails are filtered by my publisher. Good news is always welcome.

Chris Johns - **chris_johns@awesomeauthors.org**

You might also want to check my blog for Updates and interesting info.
http://chris-johns.awesomeauthors.org/

About the Publisher

4Fun Publishing, a member of **BLVNP Incorporated**, 340 S. Lemon #6200, Walnut CA 91789, info@blvnp.com / legal@blvnp.com
NOTE: Due to the highly emotional reaction of some people to works of erotic fiction, any email sent to the above address that contains foul language or religious references is automatically deleted by our anti-spam software and will not be seen. All other communications are welcome.

DISCLAIMER

Best Friends
Hot Gay Romance Erotica

By: Chris Johns

© Chris Johns 2014
ISBN: 978-1-62761-909-7

Chapter 1

"Hi, Jess, wusup?"

I couldn't remember a school morning for years when I hadn't said the same thing as I approached the school bus stop nearest my house. Jess always beat me there, and he was my best friend. He had always been my best friend.

Now that we were seniors, we hit the back seat, which was now recognized as ours by rite of passage. I would check his homework as we meandered through the local area picking up other students. Jess was the jock and I was the nerd. Not really, but I was the clever one, so I always checked his homework. That's not to say he was a dumb jock, because he wasn't…he was one very smart guy; I was just a bit more academic. I wasn't a complete nerd either; I wasn't all that sporty, but I was a runner…cross country in the winter, track in the summer. I was lean and wiry; Jess was built in a way you would expect a running quarterback to look. I don't think there was enough fat on either of us to measure. We had a good circle of friends, and I never felt out of place with his football crowd. The only way we diverged seriously was that Jess loved to party, and I was more of a homebody.

My happiest times were when Jess and I were one to one in either house. We played computer games, worked on our assignments together, or just chilled…talking about girls, sports, sex, the usual teen stuff. The only deception in our relationship, as far as I knew, was that I was gay, but Jess didn't know that, and I was just about 100% certain that Jess wasn't. He was a pussy magnet, but as far as I knew he was still a virgin. How I would love him to take my virginity, and vice versa. The weird thing was that, despite my lust for Jess, I had never seen him naked.

The best I had gotten was a look at his naked torso when he was dressed in shorts and no top. His body was to die for, and I nearly always got hard looking at it.

I guess he was having a hard time with a girlfriend one day when our relationship changed. He was as horny as hell when I dropped round to see him that day. We were crashed out in his bedroom and he was telling me all about the newest bird. She wouldn't let him get to first base.

"I haven't even felt her tits, Austin; how fucking frustrating is that? I have blue balls after every date with her, and I'm almost permanently hard. I need someone to lavish some tender loving care on my little head, preferably with a soft pussy, but a soft mouth would be nearly as good, and I wouldn't even say no to a hand job that wasn't my hand."

I laughed, but couldn't help letting my eyes wander down to look at the bulge in his shorts. Of course he noticed.

"You don't have that problem with girls do you, Bud?"

I looked up at him with surprise and guilt written across my face. I don't think I recovered it very well when I replied.

"Nah, too busy looking after you."

"Well, why don't you really look after me and uncover what your eyes were glued to, for starters?"

"You're not serious are you?"

The tone was all wrong; I sounded too eager.

"I'm serious, Austin. I know you want to, and I want you to; so no problem."

He swung round in his chair, pushed his legs out straight, about eighteen inches apart, and slid down a bit, pulling his shorts up tight and emphasizing his bulging groin.

"Hey, Buddy, you know I'd do anything for you, but if I do this, it never gets out of this room."

"Of course not; just go ahead; do what you like."

No way could I turn down this invitation. Just being able to look at him naked and hard was the stuff of dreams, and I was being invited to do more. I slid between his legs and looked up at him; he smiled and just nodded, so I undid the drawstring on his athletic shorts and started to ease them down. He lifted his butt to assist, and I edged back to allow myself to slide them right off. I gasped: his cock was clearly outlined in his boxer briefs; and it was a big one! I wasn't sure it was bigger than mine, but certainly close, and I knew I was bigger than average. I stroked it through the cotton of his briefs, and was almost drooling when I got the final go-ahead. He lifted his butt again, and I took the waistband in my two hands and eased it over his cock as I removed them. I sat back on my heels and just looked at him head to toe, especially his groin.

I looked in his eyes and almost whispered, "You look sensational, Jess."

He grinned, and, with a lustful gaze said, "Well, don't just look at it; do something with it."

I touched it very tentatively. He didn't say anything, so I took it in my hand and started slowly jacking him. He gave a huge sigh of pleasure and slid down his chair more, opening his legs wider. I got bolder and used my other hand to play with his balls. He loved that as well. It didn't take him long before he blasted his chest with a fountain of cum that must have shot at least a foot in the air. Some dribbled onto my hand as the power of his orgasm abated; and, without thinking, I put the hand to my mouth and licked it off. I looked up and realized that Jess had seen it, but he didn't say anything; he just smiled at me, leaned forward, and patted my head.

"Thanks, Bud; that was great!"

I smiled. I was so pleased I had satisfied him, and he looked pleased as well. He wiped up the cum with tissues, which he threw in his wastebasket before sliding his boxers and shorts back on. No angst, no condemnation; so I relaxed.

We carried on, playing and talking as though nothing had happened. I went home feeling relaxed, but horny as hell. I had been so hard since I jacked him off. I was ready to explode; and I did, in double quick time when I got to my room. It must have been the quickest load I ever got rid of; and what a load!

"HI, JESS, wusup?"

No change the next morning at school. He had football training that day, so I went home alone, and his mum picked him up. That was the last day I caught the school bus for a long time…the next morning I opened the front door to find a grinning Jess sat behind the wheel of a neat open top sports car.

"Your chariot awaits, Sir."

I hopped in and got the story on the way to school. His dad had brought it home the night before as a reward for his previous semester results that pushed him into the bracket where he could expect a scholarship. That would save his dad a fortune in college fees, so the car was a cheaper option.

"Now that you have a chauffeur every day, and I don't have training, I reckon you should show your appreciation in my bedroom after school today. We can do our assignments as well."

He was grinning and I joined him. I also got a tingle in my groin that became a full-blown erection. Jess noticed, and laughed. He patted it and said, "Down boy; he's got a few hours before there is anything to see."

I was happy. No recriminations. I couldn't wait for the end of school!

We got to Jess's house; no one was in, so he suggested we take a shower before doing anything else. I didn't want to because he would see my hard cock as soon as I removed my shorts and boxers. He won, of course, and accused me of being a horny little faggot. Still no animosity, so I shrugged and we showered.

He went straight to his bed and was laid on his back by the time I got to him, arms behind his head.

"Today, I want you to make it even more erotic for me than you did last time."

Well, that was going to be no problem. I was able to suck him, play with his balls, and tweak his nipples…all at the same time, by kneeling alongside the bed. His orgasm was even better than last time, even though I finished it with my hand; and, like last time, I licked his cum off my hand.

"You might as well lick the remainder off my cock, too, Austin."

I did, and shot a load over the floor without touching myself. Touching his cock again with my tongue was incredible. Jess saw it and laughed.

"So my best bud really is a little faggot. I guess he had better see if you can give me a decent blowjob next time, keeping it in your mouth to take my juice straight from the source."

I couldn't hide my pleasure at that statement, and kissed the end of his cock before falling back on my haunches and laughing.

"Oh, yes, Master! Your wish is my command."

That was the wrong thing to say, because it planted the idea in his head that governed our future relationship for ages.

Another thing I didn't realize, until much later, was that he was jealous of my cock, because it was quite a lot bigger than his, and looked more so because I was smaller in build.

Nothing changed in our relationship as far as everyone else knew, but in either of our bedrooms Jess became more dominant; blowjobs first, and they were great; then he made me rim him one day, and I nearly fainted with the pleasure of being able to attack his ass. I stroked, licked, prodded with my tongue, and brushed my cheek against it. I was in heaven, except for one thing…Jess never touched me or allowed me to have an orgasm unless it was a 'no touch' one.

"You're a little faggot, Austin, and I'm a straight jock; I can't allow you to indulge in that queer shit in front of me."

I was hurt and embarrassed, so I said nothing.

The next development was a shocker, and I should have rebelled, but I just blustered a little. One of Jess's other friends was another jock. I always thought of him as a gentle giant, which is probably why I went along with the programme Jess had planned.

It started when we arrived at Jess's house after school one day. Cody was waiting for us.

"Cody's girlfriend has just ditched him so I thought we could cheer him up."

I looked at Jess to see if he was planning what I thought he was. He was, and started straight away.

"Even his girlfriend never gave him a decent blowjob, Bud, so I told him my best bud would oblige to make him feel good. You will, won't you, Austin?"

I shook my head, "No, how could you? I'm not the resident cocksucker."

Jess stood in front of me, hands on hips, legs spread.

"You called me 'Master,' and have obeyed me ever since. You're my sex slave, and if you want to continue in that roll you'll be nice to my friends."

I thought about it. Ok, he never touched me, but I had free use of his incredible body almost as frequently as I wished; I couldn't lose that; it was too important for my psyche. You see, I knew that I loved Jess. So, I hung my head and just whispered, "Yes, Master."

"Good boy. Now strip; slaves shouldn't have clothes on in front of their masters."

I didn't argue; there was no point. I knew I would do what he wanted, in the end. I felt acute embarrassment standing in front of Cody, naked.

"Good boy. Now take him through to my bedroom and pleasure him. I'll be out here, Cody. If he doesn't measure up, you can plaster his butt with a few good slaps to make him perform better. He is the best cock sucker I know, so don't accept second best."

I wondered how quickly Jess would kill my love for him. *Pretty damn quick,* I thought, *if he extended his control much further.* He looked like a pussycat with his soft brown hair and lovely full kissable lips, but he was beginning to show me he wasn't.

Cody was different…like chalk and cheese. He had jet-black hair and almost black eyes, but they were surprisingly gentle eyes, which surprised me. His lips were full and kissable, as well, but had a firmer set. He was gently spoken, and I warmed to him despite the situation.

"I've never had another guy touch me before, Austin, so why don't you tell me what to do. I just want to get my rocks off; I don't care how, so even a hand job will feel great, I'm sure."

I looked at him to see if he was teasing, but it didn't look like it.

"I think I can probably do better than that, Master."

Cody touched my cheek to get my attention.

"You don't have to call me Master, Austin; I'm just Cody."

I needed to keep this professional or my embarrassment and shame would hinder things.

"Yes I do. Jess controls me because I love him, but I can only do this for you if I do it as a slave. Now just stand there while I undress you."

I made it as erotic as I could and was rewarded with a cock to die for when I slid his boxer briefs off…still smaller than mine, but not by much, and perfect. He had a lovely prominent glans, which I was going to punish with my tongue. The ball sac, even with him being erect, was loose enough to pleasure, but not too loose. I made him go to the bed and lay down.

"I know I am doing this to order, Master, but you are stunning and I can't wait to play with that beautiful cock and balls."

I could see that he was very pleased with my comment, so I decided I would give him the best blowjob I could. I stroked his body first and licked bits that appealed to me, like his nipples. I had never done that to Jess, but I wanted to with Cody. I spread his legs, got between them, and spent ages licking his inner thighs and his ball sac. I used a hand to hold his balls up and ran my tongue over the area behind them. He was so turned on by that he bent his legs, exposing his perineum, so I licked that as well. He gasped and I looked up to his eyes. They had gone all dreamy, and he reached down, stroked my hair, and almost whispered to me.

"That is fantastic, Austin, don't stop!"

Hell, I always do as I'm told; well, when it suits me, and this suited me. He was delightful to play with; much more responsive than Jess.

It must have been fifteen to twenty minutes after I started before I actually touched his cock. I licked base to tip on the underside before levering it away from his abdomen and licked that gorgeous glans. I gradually swallowed all of him, testing my gag reflex before sliding back up to work some more on his glans while I played with his balls. I was in cock heaven as I felt him swell before unloading a huge volume of cum in my mouth. I loved it and sucked him dry, still gently fondling his balls and inside thighs as he came down from his high. I came off his cock, eventually, and sat back on my haunches.

When he focused on me again, he smiled and said, "I have never had an orgasm like that in my life, Austin. It was truly amazing. Let me get you off now."

I looked shocked! I couldn't imagine one of these straight jocks offering to touch my cock. I blustered a little, by which time Cody had swung forward and had taken my cock in his hand and started to jack me. I thought he was going to take it in his mouth, but I was so turned on by him that I orgasmed before he got there.

"I'm sorry, Master; you were just so exciting I couldn't hold it."

I was shattered then when he moved closer and kissed me on the lips. I thought I was going to die; it was so unexpected and so sensational.

"Nothing to apologize for. I think you are amazing. I hope we can do this, and more sometime."

He hopped out of bed, got dressed and left me. I heard him tell Jess that I was just what he needed, and then I heard the door close, and Cody's car was backing out of the drive. Jess came into the bedroom and looked at my soft cock, and all the cum spread over his bed.

"You messy bastard, Austin, what's all this?"

I was still recovering and just told him, "Cody was so sexy I came almost the same time as him." I wasn't going to tell him Cody had done it.

"Well you had better clean it up, and then I'm going to punish you. Little faggots are here to please me and my mates; not to get off themselves."

Being best friends appeared to be something in the past, but I felt strong enough to ask.

"I don't qualify any more as your best friend then Jess?"

He looked at me as though appraising a piece of livestock.

"You'll know the answer to that after I've finished punishing you."

I changed the sheets on his bed, put the dirty ones in the laundry baskets, and looked round the bedroom. It was all neat and tidy. Jess came in then with a self-satisfied smirk on his face.

"I've decided that as you love my cock so much you will be denied it for two weeks. You are also to desist from jacking off during that time. Don't think you can cheat because I will know when I next allow you to cum; besides, I will see your almost permanent hard on when you can't relieve yourself. Also, I've been told that fucking boy cunt is even better than women, so I am thinking that next time I'll try that. But for now, this should teach you to know your place. You aren't supposed to cum when you are pleasuring my guests."

I took that to read that Cody wasn't going to be the last.

"I want you back here in two weeks' time. I'll let you know the exact date, ready for a good fucking; so make sure you are clean inside."

I looked at him with hate filled eyes.

"I don't think so. As your best friend, I would have done anything for you. I loved you, Jess, but if you even liked me a little you couldn't do this to me. I'll survive without your cock."

He sneered. "Oh, you'll be here or everyone in school will know you're a cock sucking faggot."

That was when I realized I couldn't get out of this. I dragged myself home and cried for what I had lost. I took the bus to school, and I kept clear of the jocks.

I had two miserable weeks then. Of course, I jacked off, but it wasn't the same without the regular stimulus of sucking Jess.

"I will pick you up from school; you are coming to my house."

That was the best news I had in two weeks; and, despite the fact that he was no longer being my friend, I looked forward to resuming my time as his sex slave.

That was it; so of course I did as I was told. At Jess's house, he sent me straight to the bathroom and told me to douche first and then shower.

"When you are finished, stand in front of my chest of drawers; feet apart and hands behind your back."

I did, and it was ages before he walked in again, with Cody and another member of the football team, who I didn't know. He was some kind of idiot, I reckoned. He was still wearing his kneepads and socks. When he stripped down later, he kept those on. He was a good looking guy, with a warm smile; but, as I found out, not averse to a little rough sex. Cody didn't look comfortable, and that made me a little wary; he must know something I didn't.

"Turn round, Cocksucker, and show them your pretty butt, so that they can see what they are going to get the use of from my sex slave."

I did and I heard Cody, his voice was full of anger.

"Are you fucking crazy, Jess? A few blowjobs are fine, but this is going too far, unless Austin wants it. How can you let him use you like this, Austin?"

I turned round again with tears in my eyes.

"Because I'm his slave, and if I don't do as I'm told he will let the whole school know that I suck cock."

"Not only that, Cody, but when we have finished today, we'll also be able to add that he takes cock up his ass as well."

Jess was laughing, and Cody came back at him.

"Well you had better make sure he is treated properly, or you could damage his insides."

I'm not sure who was the most surprised at that outburst; Jess or me?

"Ok, well, let's get to it then. You can undress Johnny first, slut, and give him a blow job while I open up your ass."

Undressing didn't take long: shirt, shorts and briefs; then he sat down, legs wide open, showing a good size cock...rock hard, ready to be sucked. Jess went round the other end and started fingering me. I could see Cody out of my peripheral vision, and felt embarrassed. He was turned on enough for his bulge to be very pronounced. Johnny let me suck him for a few minutes, and then he moved forward more, gripped my head, and rough fucked my face, making me gag several times before unloading a massive orgasm in my mouth.

"Not a bad cock sucker; your turn now, Cody."

I was on all fours now, with Jess continuing to finger me. I had never felt so humiliated; nothing had ever been up inside me, and now I suddenly have a guy fucking me with four fingers.

"I'll wait, "was Cody's reply.

"Right. Cocksucker, on the bed; I think on your back."

I did, and I very quickly had my legs spread wide with Jess between them. He lubed his cock and my ass, and then, with no preamble, buried it in me. I cried out with the pain. The pain didn't last long though, and before I knew it I was sliding off to another world. He kept hitting my prostate, so I naturally got very hard.

"Huh, the cocksucker is really enjoying this; look at his shitty big cock. Hold it up for us all to see."

I did, and Johnny gasped.

"If he was a real slave, I'd cut that off; it's obscene."

Cody laughed. "You mean it's embarrassing that this little guy has several inches more than either of you macho jocks."

If looks could kill, Cody would have been dead.

Jess then fucked me for pain, and achieved it, ramming his cock into me as hard as he could until he orgasmed inside me.

"Your turn, Johnny."

I screamed with the pain from Johnny's fucking; it really was a power fuck. But that was good, because Cody stepped in then.

"That's it! Enough is enough. I'm taking this boy out of here, and I'll floor anyone that tries to stop me."

The others were too shocked to try to stop him.

"Get your clothes, Austin; we're leaving!"

I grabbed my stuff and ran to Cody's car, stark naked. Cody was close behind, and we drove away.

I still managed to see the humor in Cody's comment. We were the same age, but he was talking about me as though I was a little boy.

"Where are we going, Master?"

"Cut that crap, Austin; I'm Cody and you are no one's slave ever again!"

I didn't argue; no point. I was going to be Jess's slave for as long as he wanted; I didn't have any choice. We pulled into a covered slot at a health clinic. I was still naked, but Cody took me inside, straight to an examination room, without anyone seeing us. He left me for about five minutes, before he came back in with a man that looked old enough to be his dad.

"Up on the table, Boy, on your tummy; I'm just going to take a couple of swabs from your rectum."

I was as embarrassed as hell, letting this stranger slide little cotton buds up my ass.

"Use your cell to take some photos of his butt, son. ... Good, now where are his clothes?"

"In the car, Dad."

"Well, you go and get them while I get Sam to shower him and clean out his insides."

Fuck! This guy was a doctor, and Cody's dad, and now a total stranger was going to shower me, and, no doubt, give me a couple of douches.

That's what happened. Sam was a male nurse. He came in dressed in swim trunks and took me through to a shower with a fitted douche. I was given two before Sam washed me, completely pampering me.

"You're a good looking kid, Austin; I hope you get through this ok."

I thanked him. He had been so nice, not embarrassing me at all. By the time Doctor Staples came back, I was dressed, and Cody was talking quietly to me.

"Alright, Cody. I've cleared a night sleepover for Austin, with his parents, and you are both excused from school tomorrow. Now take this boy home, look after him, and use this in his bottom before you go to bed, and as soon as you wake up in the morning. Repeat every two hours tomorrow, and he should be fine for school the next day. He's not damaged, but his anus is distended and quite puffy, and I'm sure, sore as well."

He wasn't wrong there.

I was rendered speechless. My life for the next 24 hours was mapped out for me and I hadn't protested. Cody drove me to a beautiful mansion close by, and took me up to his bedroom. Huh, more like a ballroom; it was huge, with a sitting area as well as the bedroom part, bathroom en-suite and a walk in closet.

"Wow, Master, I'm glad I don't have to look after this!"

"You want me to be your 'master,' well fine. Now, slave, get naked."

He sounded pissed off, so I did. Hell, he had seen me naked more than he had clothed, so no point in being coy.

"Now undress me."

No problem; his gorgeous body, and a cock I knew would grow to almost match me, was not going to be difficult to undress.

"Now get on the bed on your back, hands behind your head."

Half an hour later, I was crying with happiness. This guy had taken that long to make me orgasm, almost destroying my sanity in the process.

"I wanted to do that the first time I saw you, Austin. When your bottom is all better, I hope you will let me do to you what those two animals did tonight, but I'll be doing it gently, and with love."

Love; that was a powerful word, but I couldn't speak yet. This guy was unbelievable.

We had dinner with Cody's parents and no mention was made of my earlier ordeal; to Mrs. Staples I was just a friend of her son's.

Bed came quite early, and Cody worked some more of the cream into my ass. Then, into bed, and Cody spooned me into him, kissed my neck and said goodnight.

Chapter 2

"Good morning, sexy man; ready for me to attack your ass again?"

That was my greeting as I woke up. He was waving the tube of cream around and grinning. I rolled over and let him very gently cream my ass.

"Quick wash, tooth clean, and breakfast with Mum and Dad before I bring you back here for a shower and a talk."

No problem. His Mum was a doctor as well, and they both left for work, leaving a maid to clear things away, and Cody took me back to his suite. The shower included another pampering and a very nice hand job to orgasm. I began to like this guy.

We did the assignments we should have done yesterday, and then sat in the lounge part of the bedroom while Cody told me what he hoped would happen.

"The swabs dad took from your ass will be checked for DNA against Jess and Johnny, if they try anything on. Coupled with my testimony and the photographs, we almost certainly have enough evidence to put them in jail for rape. Dad's lawyer will be apprising them of that at lunchtime. They will be informed that will only happen if they ever lay a hand on you again or breathe a word of the happenings concerning you and gay sex. So, you can resume your life any way you choose. I know you are gay, and I'm going to keep asking you for dates until you say 'yes,' because I want you to be my boyfriend."

I looked shocked.

"Are you gay, as well, Cody?"

He nodded.

"Yes, I have known since I was a kid. I'm pretty good at covering it up by having girlfriends who usually ditch me because I don't pet with them. I can just about manage a kiss and that's it. With you, I could kiss all day. I think you are pretty special, Austin."

I thought I would be cheeky then. I knew my ass was too be used by Cody to fuck me, but I felt good and wanted to get to grips with his cock again.

"Ok, I'll give you a trial as a boyfriend. The first test to see if I want to try further is for you to get naked and go lay on your bed, hands behind your head, and you aren't to move until I tell you to."

He nodded agreement, and did it. When he was lying on the bed, my eyes watered. I could have this incredibly sexy man on my terms. He was gorgeous, and the cock and balls were a dream come true to a slut like me. I couldn't wait for him to ream out my ass with it. He wasn't as thick as me, so I was sure he wouldn't hurt me.

I started by lying over his body and rubbing our groin areas together at the same time as I kissed him. He was a wonderful kisser, and I took ages to give up on that. I did tell him, between kisses, that I owed him a great deal, which I would probably never be able to repay. He smiled at me.

"You already have. That first blowjob paid for everything you could possibly owe me for life."

I grinned and slid down far enough to take his nipples in my mouth. I ground one in between my teeth, very lightly, of course, and then did the same with the other one. Ha, ha, the first very sensitive point. I continued the slide to get between his legs. He was rock hard and secreting pre-cum. I lapped it up, and licked all-round the head of his cock before going further south and taking his balls in my mouth. I bared my teeth as I looked up at him with an evil grin, and I started to bite down on his scrotum. He looked scared, until I changed my look and swabbed his balls with my tongue.

"I'll get you for that when your ass is ready for me to damage it again."

We both laughed and I slid back up the bed for some more kisses.

"I think you are a very nice man. I'm going to give very careful consideration to your request to be my boyfriend."

Of course, I was grinning as I said it. I moved back down to finish the job I started, and gave him an orgasm that made him squeal with pleasure.

"Considerations complete; I think I'll give you a three month trial."

He rolled me over onto my back and nearly took my sanity, making love to me without his cock getting anywhere near my ass.

I still had a sore ass when I went into school the next day, but I felt like a million dollars. How could I have been fooled by Jess for so many years? Cody had shown me more love in 24 hours than Jess had in 12 years. So, I had a new best friend, and I had the feeling this one was going to be around as long as Jess had been.

I wanted to go home with Cody that day, and every other day, but reality had to be faced. I went home, determined to tell my parents I was gay and had a boyfriend, who I thought might be a permanent feature in my life.

I sat mum and dad down in the lounge, when they were both home from work, and started my planned speech. "Please, Mum, Dad, what I have to say won't please you, but don't say anything until I'm finished."

I intended to hit them with the gay bit straight away. If it shocked them so much that they threw me out, it would save a lot of unnecessary words on my part.

"I'm sorry to tell you that you won't be having any grandchildren, because I'm gay."

Pause for the explosion that didn't come, they just looked at each other.

"I've always loved Jess but knew he wasn't gay, so it didn't matter about me. A few weeks ago, Jess told me that I satisfied him sexually. It got a bit out of hand and he used me badly. One of his friends became my knight in shining armor, and I fell in love with him. I know this is the real thing, so you have to know, because I want to spend a lot of time with him. His parents both know, and approve, so I'm hoping you two will at least accept me for who I am. I love you both so much, and I'll be so sorry if I can't keep your love and make you proud of me."

I sat back then and switched my eyes between the two, waiting for a reaction. I could see my dad thinking, and my mum waiting for him to say something.

"I think we should throw the little faggot out, don't you honey?"

I could see my mother's look of shock before dad continued.

"On the other hand, what would we do without our clever son?"

He looked at me with a look that said 'I love you' and then he said it.

"We'll never stop loving you, you idiot. You were conceived with love, born into love and brought up with love. We are proud of the young man you have become, and your sexuality doesn't change that. Yes, we'll be a little sad that you are gay, because life will not be as easy for you as it would otherwise; but you'll always have our support. Now, more practical things…when are we going to meet the young man that has stolen our son's heart?"

I was so relieved, I couldn't speak for a minute; then I grabbed my cell and called Cody.

"Hiya; Dad wants to know when you can come to dinner, so that he can kill you for corrupting his son."

I giggled, and my dad nearly fell off his chair laughing. Hilarity over with, and Cody was coming to dinner the next day.

"If you come home with me, we can do our assignments before Mum and Dad get in from work, to give us the whole evening together."

That was it. I briefed Cody that we were not going to discuss my sore butt, or any details of Jess's action.

I LOVED it when we were all sat in the lounge before dinner. Dad carried out a very proficient interrogation of Cody, making me curl up with laughter at some of the questions. The one that floored me was, *'what are your intentions toward my son?'* What a hoot.

Cody's answer made me sit up and look at him with a shocked look on my face.

"Totally dishonorable, Sir."

Then Cody laughed and told my parents the truth, I hoped.

"To be his best friend and partner for the remainder of my life, if he'll have me."

He looked at me, and I was lost. There was so much love in that look…I wanted to cry with happiness. Mum and dad saw it as well, and that got Cody the seal of approval.

Sleepovers at one or the other of the houses became almost the standard, even on school nights. We both got the same lecture from both sets of parents.

"We'll sanction the mid-week sleepovers, but the second your grades slip, all sleepovers will become history."

That wasn't going to happen. Together, we were acing every subject. The reason was simple: studying with the guy you love becomes fun, and we very quickly deepened our love for one another.

It must have been a month before my butt was completely normal, and Cody wouldn't touch it while there was any sign of my invasive sex. He did, however, make love to me every night we were together. It was difficult to remember that his first gay sex had been with me, because he became such an awesome lover he had me in tears frequently. Happy tears, of course.

The first time he penetrated me was incredible. I had expected it to be in bed after a long session of loving, but how it happened was mind blowing. It was at Cody's house on a Friday night. We had retired to his suite immediately after dinner, and stripped naked before sitting in the lounge area and making out. We were both rampantly erect, but Cody appeared to be another inch or so longer than normal. He was so hard. Then he jumped up, went to his bedside cabinet, and came back with a condom and a lube.

"I can't wait any longer; I'm planting little Cody where he should have been weeks ago."

He swung me round on the couch, lifted my legs onto his shoulder and using lube, very quickly, opened me up to four fingers before lubing his cock and my ass. He slid over my sphincter, with virtually no pain; but I must have looked scared, because he laughed before falling forward and kissing me passionately. I could feel him sliding further in as he kissed me, and then he started fucking me, long and slow, feeding me a little more each entry, until I could feel his pubic hair on my balls. The sensation was amazing, and my cock, that had softened a little, came back to rock hard.

Cody saw it and smiled before concentrating on what he was doing. The guy was incredible! This was his first fuck, and he behaved like a pro. He started rotating his hips as he entered, and that just blew my mind. I started orgasming, and didn't stop until Cody had a fantastic orgasm of his own. The mess of cum that Cody fell into, after his orgasm, eventually had us in hysterics when we realized what it looked like. The important thing, though, was that it had been fantastic for me. It didn't matter that it had been a quickie.

"I love you so much, Austin, I just couldn't wait any longer. Now, shower and bed, because I'm going to do that again; only this time I'm going to take until dawn."

He wasn't joking. It was daylight before we eventually fell asleep. Cody had cleaned up both of us with a warm cloth, so that I didn't have to get out of bed; but during our sleep hours, Cody's cum had leaked out of my butt. The smell of stale sex when we woke, nearly lunchtime, was awful.

Cody's dad, knocked and entered as we were stretching, prior to getting up. He wrinkled his nose, and then grinned at us as he spoke.

"You two are disgusting. You need to open some windows, change your bedding and get it in the wash before your mother comes up here. Oh, and lunch will be ready in half an hour."

Cody laughed so hard I thought he would damage himself. What great parents he had. They didn't make us feel at all embarrassed when we arrived for lunch, but his dad did wink at me, almost making me choke.

Life was good, and got better when our final results were known. We both got the college we wanted; and, yes, it was the same one. We also went on full scholarship. Jess had fared worse than expected, proving that my input had been valuable. No scholarship, and his parents weren't very well off, so he would need to work his way through; whereas Cody and I, with only spending money to find, would be taking it easy, giving us plenty of time to study. Dr. Staples bought Cody a new car for us to take to college, so we had everything we could wish for. Cody wasn't on a sport scholarship, and didn't have any pretensions about becoming a professional footballer, so we just concentrated on studying. It paid off, and we both returned home, after four years, with first class degrees.

Cody got an amazing job with an electronics firm in R&D, at a terrific salary, and I was lucky enough to get a place at a local college to complete my architectural training. Jess and Johnny had both ended up with poor degrees, having spent too much time being jocks, and partying. Neither of them found work to start with, and the gap between us socially got wider.

At 26 years old, I became a fully qualified architect, and designed the house that we built on a plot Cody's dad bought us. I was quite shocked one day to see Jess come onto the site with one of the work gangs. I was as nice as pie to him. There was no point in being antsy; it was, after all, his actions that got me Cody. I don't think he knew Cody and I were still together, and he certainly didn't know that this was my house and not just my design.

All became clear that lunchtime. Cody drove up to the site in his new SUV and parked it alongside my Corvette. He walked over, gave me a hug and a, "Hi, Babe; ready for some lunch?"

Jess saw it; how could he not; he was only about ten feet from us, and had watched Cody pull up.

"Fuck, you two faggots are still together."

Cody made me laugh. He looked at Jess and spoke at him.

"Watch your tongue, boy, or I'll have you off this site in double quick time."

Jess sneered at him, "Fuck off, queer boy; you don't have any authority here."

Cody looked at me. "Haven't you told him that this is our new house?"

Jess gulped as Cody turned to him again.

"Give me any more lip and you'll be off this site so fast your feet won't touch the ground. Don't take any shit from him, Austin. I know he was your best friend, but he gave up all rights to that title years ago."

I grinned and replied, "Ok, Tiger; now, let's go for lunch."

Jess pussyfooted around me after that, and I almost felt sorry for him. So much unrealized potential because he was a shit. We saw him with Johnny one night at one of the seedier bars. They were outside smoking and drinking as Cody and I drove past on our way to a black tie do. What a difference to how it should have been.

Chapter 3

Cody and I had been in the new house for about a year. I was now so well established designing high-end houses, that I started cherry picking other companies personnel. I had a crew of top-flight artisans, and even my laborers were partly skilled. I paid top wages, because I demanded top quality work.

Unusual for an architect to have his own workers, but it was starting to pay off. I had to employ a project manager, because I was so busy in the office that I couldn't be on site as much as I wanted to.

Cody and I were chilling out one night at home when the doorbell rang. I answered it and facing me was a very dejected Jess, looking pretty shabby.

"Hello, Jess, what can I do for you?"

"Please, Austin, can we talk?"

He looked pathetic, so I invited him in. We went through to the study, and, on the way, I poked my head into the lounge and told Cody that Jess was here and we were going to the study to talk. I received an odd look from Cody, and I continued into the study.

"Ok, Jess, what's this all about?"

"I am pretty desperate for a job, and I hoped you could give me one."

"I'm sorry you're desperate, Jess, but you must know I employ only top flight people."

"I know, but I reckon I'm good enough to assist one of your electricians."

I was surprised. This guy was a graduate, albeit with a rotten degree, but electrician's assistants were usually kids with nothing more than a general certificate.

"In that case, you shouldn't have a problem getting a job with one of the other construction outfits or a private contractor."

"They all say I'm too old and must be a waste of space to be in this position."

"Let me bring Cody in on this."

I quickly filled Cody in before we both went back to the study. Cody asked Jess a load of questions he would have expected an electrician to know the answers to, and was surprised that Jess did.

"Jess, just go out into the entrance hall for a minute while I have a word with Austin." He went as meek as a lamb.

"He could be good, Babe; his knowledge base is sound. In the right hands, he might even make it as a proper electrician in a couple of years. We know he's not stupid; just not motivated enough to do well at college. You could do a lot worse than employ him, but if you take him on, why don't you use a little blackmail. I'm sure he'd love to give us blowjobs occasionally, and maybe even take it up the ass to get and keep a job."

I was shocked to start with, and then amused.

"Mmm, I could have him in between my legs giving me a blowjob while I thought about it."

Well, that was it. Jess was called back in and stood in front of my desk. Cody left, and I looked at my former best friend.

"I think I might be able to use you, Jess, provided you fit my parameters. So, to start with, would you like to get undressed so that I can have a look at what I'm considering employing?"

He blustered, of course, but when I indicated he could go, he became very cooperative. He still looked good when he was naked. A little soft round the middle, but I guessed that was the beer.

"Not bad, but you are already going to pot, Jess; too much beer, I guess. If I employ you, I will expect to see that softness disappear very quickly."

"Oh yes, Austin; no problem."

"Good, but I think you should drop the 'Austin,' as I'm the boss. 'Sir' will do in the future."

He looked ready to rebel again, until he saw my look.

"Yes, Sir."

I knew he hated that.

"Good. Now, while I think about this, why don't you undress me as well, and then you can give me a blowjob while I think."

He looked shocked, and sealed his fate.

"I'm not a faggot; I don't suck cock."

"Well, you might as well get dressed then, because my assistant electrician will suck mine and Cody's cocks whenever we want, and also take our cocks up his ass."

Jess was so straight, I thought; he had a raging battle going on in his head. He was desperate for a job, but hated the idea of a reversal of his previous sexual relationship with me; again, I had it all wrong.

"I can't, that is so queer."

Easy for me, and I said, "Ok, good bye."

I stood up and he moved in front of me and started undressing me. When I was naked, and sat comfortably again, he started giving me a blowjob. Pretty useless, so I started teaching him. He kept looking up at me hoping I would let him off. I didn't, and took great satisfaction out of cumming in his mouth, and making him swallow it.

"That wasn't very good, but here's the deal I'm prepared to offer you. I'll give you a 90-day trial."

Amazing how good things turned out for me with 90 day trials, I hoped this one would as well.

"Every Friday you will come to the house after work for me to see the improvements in your body, and Cody and myself will teach you how to give good head, and we'll keep your other end well opened up by fucking you as well. Standard salary for my crew; no negotiation; take it or leave it."

He looked at me to see if I might bend, saw the determined look, and nodded his head. I briefed him on where he should be, and to whom he should report.

"Be warned, Jess, you will have to be better than anyone else if you want to keep the job, this is payback." He nodded, got dressed and left. Cody was rocking with laughter when I told him.

"Great! He was always a sexy bastard; I'll have no problem fucking him silly."

Cody and I had a wonderful loving relationship and had never sought outside stimulation or satisfaction. He was, to me, the perfect mate, and I guess I was for him, so it would be a new experience for us to have threesomes, and even one on ones with Jess.

I must be going soft, because, in discussion with Cody, we decided that we would only teach him to give good head for a few weeks before attacking his backend. I kept close tabs on him at work, talking to his supervisor almost every day.

"Honestly, Boss, he is the best assistant I have ever had. He's very intelligent, and seldom needs telling anything twice. If you really want to get the best out of him, I would suggest you day release him to the local tech college to do the theory, and you would have another qualified electrician very quickly. Pretty useful with your rate of expansion."

I guess I was pleased with that assessment from my senior site electrician. I know Jess had been a bastard after he found out I was gay, but he really had been a best friend for so many years. Of course, I relayed all this to Cody. That was when I saw the depths to which Cody would go to make me happy.

"Know that whatever you want to do with Jess is ok with me, lover. I know he was your best friend. I think we should definitely continue the present plan, graduating to reaming him out a few times; but if you want to lay off him, then I don't have a problem; and sending him to tech makes sense as well. You can't afford not to make the most of all your employees." I hopped into his lap then, and buried him in kisses.

"You must have read my mind." Which I'm sure he did often.

"I can't keep being beastly to him, Cody. I guess the years of him being a great guy have to count for something. How about we finish his training as a cock sucker, and then spend just a few weeks reaming out his ass before releasing him from that side of his employment?"

"Ok by me, Babe."

The next Friday, I told Cody I was going to take Jess to a guest bedroom and get him to make love to me, without the penetration of course. If he was good, I was going to get him to do the same to Cody, and then the next week we would take on his ass. Agreement reached, and when Jess arrived, I took him straight through to a guest bedroom, which was also en-suite.

"We are going to shower first, Jess, because I want you to make love to me tonight, and I may reciprocate if you are enthusiastic. Of course, there is to be no penetration; that is, unless you are incredibly good," and I grinned.

His body had tightened up quite well during his time with me, and seeing him naked as we went for a shower, stirred the old lust I had for him years ago. We pampered each other in the shower, and he got a serious hard on, as did I.

"My supervisor has good things to say about you, Jess, so I'm going to release you to Tech College one day a week to get your paper qualifications."

That put him in a good mood; so, when we got to the bed, he did more than just give me a blowjob. My nipples and balls were worked over as well, and he got me excited enough for me to go 69 with him. He was even more enthusiastic then, and went further than expected. He started working on my ass. He was good; he fingered me gently while still working my cock and balls. In the end, I was so turned on I told him to fuck me to orgasm. Jeez, he was good. I had a mighty orgasm, and took him with me.

"That was great, Jess, but Cody is going to kill both of us when I tell him."

Jess looked frightened, until I laughed. "Only kidding. He'll be fine."

Cody was surprised but not upset. He had, after all, started our relationship with a similar scenario.

"Next Friday, I think we should be together and get him opened up enough so that we can both fuck him, or maybe just spit roast him."

Well, that was it; Jess was in a good mood when he came to the house, because he had started tech and realized his life had started to have direction. I guess I was flavor of the month. I wasn't sure I would be when we finished, but if he played along with us, I was going to make this the last session where I made him have sex with us. I wanted him to be a useful and loyal employee for me, not a sex toy.

We started by giving Jess a double douche. Of course he hated it, but when I reminded him of all the good things that were happening to him now, he calmed down and cooperated. On the bed, I told him to get on all fours, before making him drop his head and shoulders onto the bed and spread his legs wide. I told him to slide his butt back a little, and he was in the perfect position for what I wanted. Cody climbed up onto the bed and straddled Jess, holding him still by gripping him at the waist with his calves.

"I'm going to open you up now, Jess, before planting my cock in your ass. If you are good, Cody will do the same, and if we both enjoy it, I'll have a reward for you at the end of the evening."

I was surprised. He didn't say a word. I truly expected a load of pleading, until I actually started fingering him. I pulled the first finger out and told Cody to use his hands to spread Jess's cheeks more. I gave Cody a cockeyed look, but didn't say anything. It only took me a few minutes to get to four fingers. Jess was so relaxed and already quite open. I knew that he wasn't an anal virgin, and, more than that, my guess was that he was regularly having his ass reamed out. I lubed us both and because I hadn't been touched, I managed to last quite a long time, using long slow strokes. No doubt about it, my ex best friend was proving a great fuck. Jess came twice before he took me over the top for a terrific orgasm.

"You might as well replace me straight away lover."

Cody grinned and slipped off the bed.

"Turn over Jess; I want to see your eyes as I slide into you."

While Cody was getting settled, I slid into the bathroom and cleaned my genitals, because I was going to get a blowjob. Cody was just entering Jess when I got back, and I watched his eyes. That was it; I realized that Jess was gay. No straight man would have the look that he had as Cody's monster slid into him. I moved in close and, without any prompting, Jess took me in his mouth. The result was easily the best spit roast I had ever been involved in. Jess patently loved being fucked, and that really threw me. His early reluctance had obviously been show. All finished, and we had another shower, with Cody and I pampering Jess. All dressed and, in the lounge with drinks, I grinned at Jess and spoke.

"Someone has been devious. That someone has pretended not to like gay sex, but he has been taking cock in his ass very regularly I am guessing, and I realized tonight just how good his blow jobs are."

He had the good grace to blush.

"Sorry, Austin. I didn't want you to know that I am gay, the same as you and Cody. I found out by accident one day when Johnny and I were fooling around. I lost a bet, and Johnny took my anal virginity. I realized that I loved it, and he's been doing it ever since. I don't think he's gay, but he does reciprocate with a blowjob occasionally."

Well, I just fell about laughing.

"I was going to tell you tonight that you needn't come again for sex. Now I suppose I'd better say that you can still come up here on a Friday but only if you want to."

Jess was grinning and replied, "I might just do that, Boss."

That was it. I saw him out and returned to see Cody shaking his head and muttering, "I don't believe it."

I was rather pleased. Jess had, after all, been my best friend for a lot of years. I know he was pretty evil when he discovered I was gay, but that only covered a short time. Now he was back to being the Jess I knew and loved.

"No more punishment sessions, Cody, so do we knock it on the head completely, or shall we indulge if he comes back?"

Cody grinned and said, "Whatever you like, lover, as long as you only love me and you don't get heavy with Jess." I hopped into his lap and gave him a big sloppy kiss.

"I might start to love him again, but I'm in love with you and that is never going to change."

It didn't and I had a wonderful lover for years, and a best friend who I fucked, and vice versa, for a lot more years as well. Jess got all his paper qualifications and, mainly I suppose, because he was pretty intelligent, he eventually became my senior project manager as projects kept coming my way. Cody continued with his company and eventually headed up research and development as a senior VP.

Not a very pleasant start to my gay life. But Cody and I made up for that by remaining lovers forever.

The End

Here is a sample from another story you may enjoy:

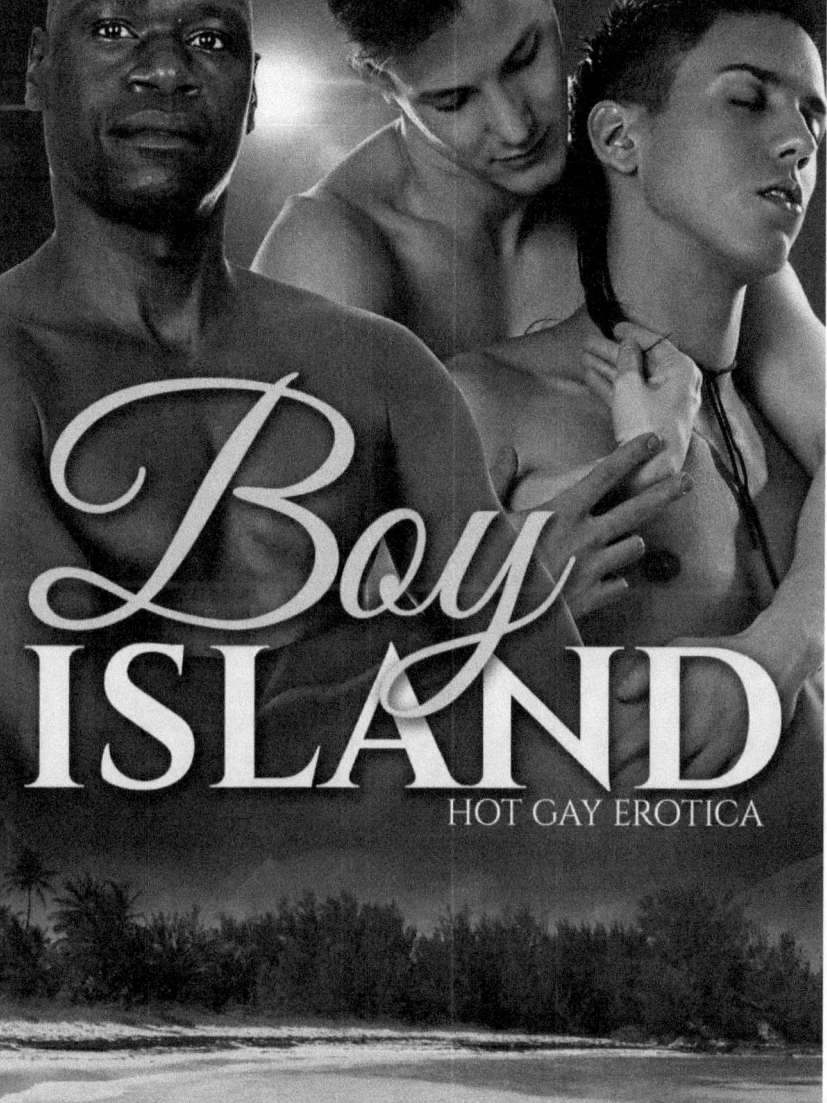

Boy ISLAND

HOT GAY EROTICA

CHRIS JOHNS

"GOOD, my name is Junior. I'm the boss boy here so you call me Master at all times, understand?"

Topha nodded.

"My cohorts are all trained warriors to protect wimps like you from the other lot. You call them Sir, understand?"

Topha was no wimp and was going to make that clear straightaway.

"I'm no wimp. They can kiss my ass before I call them Sir."

"Ok, no problem." Junior nodded.

Four boys were on Topha before he had time to react stripping him of his shorts. They pinned him face down and Junior nodded at the black warrior. He discarded his loincloth and fisted himself to an erection. Topha watched and then, as he moved round behind him he realized what was going to happen. He struggled like hell until someone grabbed his balls and squeezed hard. Result was compliance but the scream as his anus was pierced by the black rod could be heard all over the island. He was fucked until the black stud orgasmed inside him and then all of the warriors kissed his ass cheek before releasing him.

"They have all kissed your ass. Now you call them Sir, but first, you thank Leo for putting you in your place. You'll be our fuck slut until we decide if you are worth something better."

Topha was almost traumatized by his ass-fucking but did as he was told. He had never felt pain like he had just endured until his ass adapted to the invasion.

He eyed up Leo who looked older than the others.

"Yes Topha, take a good look. Leo is our champion, the oldest inhabitant of the island. He can fuck more ass in one session than anyone else, piss me off again and we will get him to try to beat his previous record, but just using you."

That was good enough for Topha. He was now determined to comply with any order whatever it was. He didn't want that black monster roaming around inside him again.

Leo was a typical black with short tight curly hair, some hair on his chest and legs and in the center a cock that had to be a good ten inches long, maybe more. He had a good body and looked to be about thirty, odd as this was supposed to be 'Boy Island'

Stood again he felt too much shame to look at any of the other warriors. He was marched back to the enclosure and saw what was going to be his home for the next two years. It looked like a mediaeval village in England. He remembered from his history books what they looked like. Shown to a hut, he was introduced to another naked boy.

"Damian, look after the new boy. Clean him up and have him at my hut in two hours' time."

Damian scanned Topha with his eyes before speaking.

"I'm Damian, I see you were the same as me, got stroppy with the Master. I suppose Leo fucked you."

Topha looked at this boy and decided he was going to like him.

"Hello, I'm Topha, and you're right. A painful introduction to my new life."

"Well, I've got two hours to try and help you not get any more punishment. Come on, let's get you showered. The two things we have plenty of here are water and soap."

Damian was eighteen, the same as Topha, mixed race, medium build with a very prominent penis. Below the waist he was quite hairy but there was little above. Topha noticed the cock because it had started to get hard.

"Sorry Topha. I love colored guys and you are pretty special to look at."

"Are you queer then?"

"Huh, everyone is queer on this island, or they're celibate, and there aren't many of them. Who do you think we are going to have sex with?"

Topha blushed. This was not what he expected at all.

"After we shower I have to give you lessons in how to suck cock unless you are already good at it."

"No way Jose, I don't suck cock."

Damian looked at this boy and wondered if he would be given to the Premier Clan.

"The Master will have you strung up and whipped before he lets Leo loose on you again unless you do as he asks. He will want you to give him a blowjob when I take you to him. If you aren't very good you will know pain like you've never known before."

Less and less Topha liked this place. He wanted to rebel again in the shower when Damian started washing his ass, particularly down the crack.

"I have to do this in case the Master wants to fuck you as well."

"I'm going to survive here Damian so I guess I have to go along with whatever they want."

Damian patted Topha's cheek. "Good boy. The better you are, the more likely they are to be gentle with you. But be prepared for a load of humiliation to start with as well as some pretty rough sex. And pray for a new boy to come quickly so that he can take your place."

If you enjoyed this sample then look for **Boy Island.**

Also by this Author:

Brotherly Love

Underworld

Revenge of the Jocks

Indian Abduction

Pleasurable Abduction

Lost

A Grip in Deep

Bullet Holes

Gay Porn Star

Delightfully Yours

Embracing the Greener Side

Promotional Desire

Aviator's Hidden Turbulence

Almost Paradise

The Hardcore Remedy

Relish Pretender

Doctor Boner

Captivated Attractions

Academically Horny

Flight of the Hornies

From the Author

If you want any more info about me, please feel free to ask! I'm a very open person so you won't offend me if you want to get more personal.

If you'd like to give me comments or suggestions to any of my books, feel free to shoot me an email at chris_johns@awesomeauthors.org.

Check my page on Amazon and my blog for Updates and interesting info.

Author Central – http://amzn.to/185Sar5
Author Blog - http://chris-johns.awesomeauthors.org/

If you enjoyed any of my books then please share the love and click like on my books in Amazon.

If you write me a review and send me an email I will send you a free book, or many.
(Just know that these emails are filtered by my publisher.)

Good news is always welcome.

One Last Thing, For Kindle Readers...

When you turn the page, Kindle will give you the opportunity to rate this book and share your thoughts on Facebook and Twitter. If you enjoyed my writings, would you please take a few seconds to let your friends know about it? Because... when they enjoy they will be grateful to you and so will I.

Thank You!

Chris Johns
chris_johns@awesomeauthors.org

About the Author

The author has drawn from his lifetime experiences as a Marine Engineer and Helicopter Pilot to take his readers round the world with his erotic stories.

Born in a small town in middle England he joined the Royal Navy straight from school and spent four years at engineering college before going to sea. After promotion to first engineer he took a career turn and trained as a helicopter pilot. The move afforded him huge opportunity to travel both as a Naval Pilot and later as a Commercial Helicopter Pilot. His Bio Pic was taken when he was relaxing in his company's social club, serving his fellow pilots and engineers with some excellent English Ale.

Retired now in the Caribbean, he took up writing to compliment his other great love, sailing.